Story By
Heather Ripkowski

Pictures By
Serena Lewis

Rainbow Baby

For rainbow babies
and angel babies
everywhere.

First printing, 2019.

I am a rainbow baby.
That's what my parents say.
A miracle from up above
Sent down to laugh and play.

One day I asked,"What does that mean?"
My mommy smiled wide.
I saw a tear roll down her cheek
And this was her reply.

"A rainbow baby is a lot of things
And so special inside.
A precious gift to your Daddy and me.
Let me tell you why."

"RED is for radiant.
You were glowing with delight.
From then on we knew
We'd always hold you tight."

"ORANGE is for outsmarting
All the odds that came to be.
You were big and strong
And grew as quickly as a weed!"

"YELLOW is for yearning.
Our smiles wouldn't fade.
We stared at the calendar
Counting down the days."

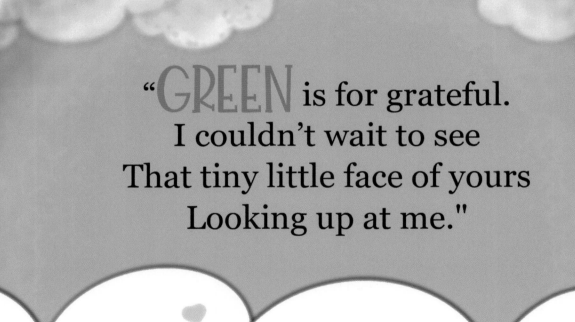

"GREEN is for grateful.
I couldn't wait to see
That tiny little face of yours
Looking up at me."

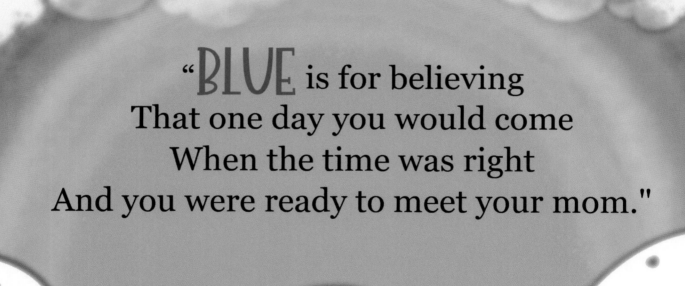

"BLUE is for believing
That one day you would come
When the time was right
And you were ready to meet your mom."

"**INDIGO** is for incredible
As cute as cute can be.
So adorable in fact
That Mommy could never leave."

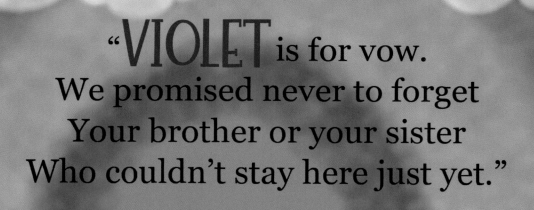

"VIOLET is for vow.
We promised never to forget
Your brother or your sister
Who couldn't stay here just yet."

"And though we miss them dearly
We know that they sent you.
Our little miracle baby
To always see us through."

Being a rainbow baby
Is more special than I knew.
I was chosen up above
Especially by you.

Even though I can't see them
We will never be apart
Because my sibling up in Heaven
Will always be in my heart.

Printed in Great Britain
by Amazon

21760807R00016